THE INCAL 1

Alexandro Jodorowsky
Jean "Moebius" Giraud
co – creators

Jean-Marc Lofficier
Randy Lofficier
translators/editors
Starwatcher Graphics

Robbin Brosterman
designer

Margaret Clark
Steve Buccellato
editors

Claudine Giraud
David Scroggy
consulting editors

Archie Goodwin
editor in chief

The Dark Incal
Yves Chaland
colors

Jim Novak
Phil Felix
letterers

The Bright Incal
Isabelle
Beaumenay-Joannet
colors

Jim Novak
Bill Oakley
Phil Felix
letters

with special thanks to
Salvador Soldevila,
Bruno Lecigne, Isabelle Morin,
Edward Magalong, & Marie Javins

The Incal 1

published by
Epic Comics
387 Park Avenue South
New York, NY 10016
ISBN # 0-87135-436-5

The Incal began in the mind of cult film-maker Alexandro Jodorowsky. (A biography of this remarkable creator will appear in the second volume of this trilogy.)

In 1975, after the success of his two motion pictures **El Topo** and **The Holy Mountain,** Jodorowsky returned to Paris to work on the film adaptation of Frank Herbert's science-fiction best-seller, **Dune.** In those pre-**Star Wars** days, it was unusual for film directors to call on outsiders such as science-fiction illustrators or comic-book artists to assist them. Yet, Jodorowsky was nothing if not unusual. He assembled an international team of uniquely talented artists, including Moebius, H. R. Giger, Chris

Foss and Dan O'Bannon.

Unfortunately, the financial backing required for this colossal project never fully materialized, and the film was abandoned. But as is always the case with such an enterprise, like an underground stream, the creative energy that had been gathered found other channels in which to express itself. O'Bannon took Giger and Moebius with him to work on **Alien.** Jodorowsky and Moebius began working on **The Incal.**

The Dark Incal first appeared in 1980. It was the first in a series of five "books". Moebius' unusual collaboration with Jodorowsky had produced a unique graphic novel, one where both story and art are literally teeming with subtext and references, clearly anticipating more recent trends in comics, both here and in Europe.

The French fans, however, had to wait eight years to discover the end of the story, since the last "book", **The Fifth Essence,** was only completed by Moebius a few months ago. The series, which was published in France in six volumes, is presented here, in its totality for the first time, as a trilogy.

And it begins here, not with a bang, but a whimper.

Jean-Marc & Randy Lofficier

BOOK ONE
THE DARK INCAL
CHAPTER ONE
CRIMSON CIRCLE NIGHTS

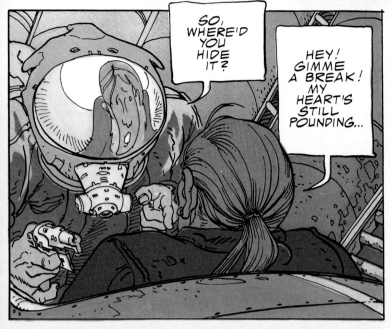

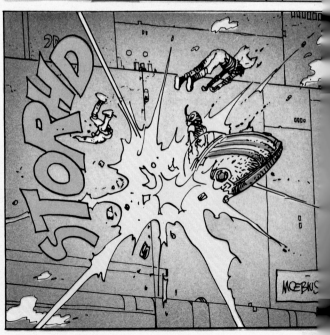

SO, THAT NIGHT, I TOOK HER TO CRIMSON CIRCLE. AND EVEN LOWER... SHE WAS INSATIABLE. I'VE GOT TO SAY THAT, WHEN IT CAME TO PARTYING, SHE KNEW HER STUFF. ANYWAY, EVERYTHING WAS LOOKING JUST FINE WHEN SHE DECIDED SHE WANTED TO FINISH UP THE EVENING WITH A BANG AT THE "DAREDEVIL." THAT'S WHERE SHE MET KILL WOLFHEAD.

YOU, BIG WOLF!

MMM...KILL, YOU KNOW HOW TO WAKE UP THE ANIMAL IN ME!

MY LADY!

KILL MUST NOT HAVE BEEN USED TO PICKING UP HER CLASS OF ARISTOS, BECAUSE HE MADE A BIG PLAY FOR HER!

ONLY TEN MINUTES LEFT.

EXCUSE ME... 'Y QUINQ, ASE... ONLY MINUTES MIDNIGHT... TIME GO!

BUT NOTHING DOING! IF THAT CRAZY WOMAN KEPT ON LIKE THAT, I COULD KISS MY FIFTY CUBLARS GOOD-BYE!

CRIPES! I'VE GOT TO FIND A WAY...

OOUUUUUU

"...AND WITH KILL'S LEGENDARY STAYING POWER, I COULD BE HERE ALL NIGHT.

EEDED TO USE ONGER TACTICS.

"IT WAS ONLY SECONDS BEFORE MIDNIGHT. MY SHOT HAD TO BE ACCURATE.

IF ONLY HE DIDN'T MOVE SO MUCH!

SHIT! THAT ASS-HOLE JUST BLASTED A HOLE IN MY EAR!

LET ME EXPLAIN, KILL! I HAVE A CONTRACT WITH THE LADY THERE. SHE PAID ME TO...

STONN!

THE BASTARD! JUST WHEN I WAS ABOUT TO COME! KILLY, MY WOLF, SKIN THAT SHITHEAD ALIVE!

MŒBIUS
6

GRRR!

THE... THE GIRL!

WHAT ABOUT HER?

KILL HIM, WOLF! I WANT HIS SKIN! I WANT ...RHAAA... AARGH! COUGH! COUGH!

MY GOD!

"IN THE FINAL ANALYSIS, NIMBEA SUPER QUINQ WAS JUST ANOTHER RICH OLD HAG WHOSE HOLOMAKEUP POWERED OFF AT MIDNIGHT!

YOU'RE ALL BASTARDS, YOU SONS OF BITCHES!

"KILL WOLFHEAD'S FRENZIED LOVE-MAKING HAD MADE THE SORDID CINDERELLA LOSE HER HEAD AND FORGET THE TIME."

WHAT'S THE RELATION BETWEEN YOUR STORY AND WHAT HAPPENED LATER AT SUICIDE ALLEY?

WELL, WOLFHEAD WENT CRAZY. HE THOUGHT I WAS RESPONSIBLE FOR WHAT HAD HAPPENED TO NIMBEA. HE STARTED TO CHASE ME THROUGH THE CROWD AT "DAREDEVIL".

THERE WAS SOMETHING ELSE, TOO. HE SHOUTED THAT HE WAS GOING TO TEAR OFF MY EARS AND MAKE ME EAT THEM!

"BUT I MANAGED TO ESCAPE THROUGH A VENTILATION SHAFT. KIL WAS JUST TOO BIG TO FOLLOW ME

"AN HOUR LATER, I WAS COMPLETELY LOST.

"WHEN, SUDDENLY, I HEARD LOU FOOTSTEPS RACING THROUGH THE HUGE, STINKING TUNNEL."

COULD I BE KILL

WHAT'S THAT?!

"I HAD NEVER SEEN OR HEARD OF SUCH A MONSTER! HE CAME AT ME LIKE A BULL-DOZER, WITH THE SAME FRIENDLY EXPRESSION ON HIS FACE!"

BUT, LUCKY ME, THE HUGE HULK WAS THERE JUST TO ONLY COLLAPSE AND DIE AT MY FEET.

"THE SHOCK WAS SO VIOLENT THAT I FAINTED DEAD AWAY!

"I JUST HAD THE TIME TO NOTICE A WEIRD BLADE STUCK IN THE MONSTER'S BACK."

EN I WOKE UP, I WAS IN IDE ALLEY WITH THOSE EE GOONS BEATING ME YOU KNOW THE REST.

ND, NATURALLY, U'D NEVER MET EM BEFORE. D YOU HAVE O IDEA AT THEY ANTED.

HECK, NO! NO IDEA! BESIDES, THEY WORE MASKS, AND...

DON'T STRAIN YOURSELF. WE'VE IDENTIFIED THEM. SMALL FRY ASSASSINS REGISTERED WITH *AMOK*. IMPOSSIBLE TO FIND OUT WHO HIRED THEM. YOU'RE FREE TO GO, DIFOOL, BUT YOU REALLY SHOULD TELL US THE TRUTH. YOU KNOW THIS CASE STINKS, AND ALL YOU'RE GOING TO GET IS..

BUT I *HAVE* TOLD YOU THE TRUTH! I HAVE NOTHING TO HIDE, PY! BESIDES, YOU CAN CHECK *EVERYTHING* I TOLD YOU: THE OLD HAG, KILL, THE MONSTER, ETCETERA...

YEAH... IT'S THAT "ETCETERA" THAT STINKS, DIFOOL!

"PY WAS PROBABLY RIGHT... BUT BY THEN, I ONLY WANTED TO GET CLEANED UP, AND FIND SOMETHING TO SMOKE AND WET MY WHISTLE, PREFERABLY IN COMPANY OF SOMEONE SOFT, CUDDLY AND PINK!"

"LATER, IN A SHOPPING GALLERY IN THE FRENCH QUARTER."

AH! THAT'S JUST WHAT I NEED!

8
MOEBIUS

CHAPTER TWO
THE INCAL'S BALL

"SHIT! WHO'D HAVE THOUGHT THAT THE VENTILATION SHAFTS OF THIS FRIGGIN' CITY WERE SO CROWDED?!"

OUTSTA!

...AND I BET THESE ARE THE GUYS WHO KINDLY DID THE PINNING!

OUTSTAAAAA

"EACH ONE OF THESE CHARMING GENTS MUST HAVE EASILY WEIGHED IN AT 800 POUNDS."

ZZTOMPP!!

NO NEED TO SHOUT LIKE THAT!

"FORTUNATELY, I HAD SOMETHING TO CALM THEM DOWN. I SET MY VIPER TO "MOB CONTROL" AND SWEPT THEM ALL WITH A CLEAN STUN BEAM. I DIDN'T EVEN NEED TO AIM."

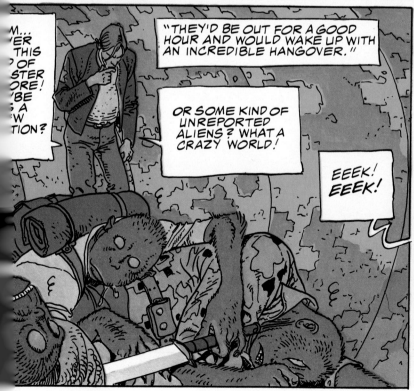

M... ER THIS OF STER ORE! BE A W TION?

"THEY'D BE OUT FOR A GOOD HOUR AND WOULD WAKE UP WITH AN INCREDIBLE HANGOVER."

OR SOME KIND OF UNREPORTED ALIENS? WHAT A CRAZY WORLD!

EEEK! EEEK!

"THE REAL SURPRISE CAME WHEN I NOTICED THAT MY "BUTTERFLY" WAS STILL ALIVE... AND THAT HE SPOKE CITIZEN LIKE YOU AND ME..."

WITH JUST A TRACE OF LOWER-LEVEL ACCENT...

11

IT WAS A SMALL BOX, NOTHING SPECIAL, EXCEPT FOR A STRANGE, TINGLING SENSATION.

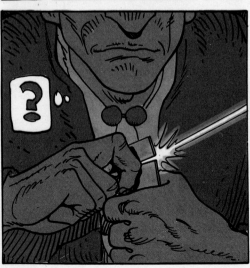

...N, A FOURTH, EN MORE GHTENING, OTAGONIST ERGES OM THE 'S DEPTHS...

THIS IS INSANE!

KEEP MOVING!

LOOK! A COMBAT ROBOT!

DEAR VIDFANS, A REAL WAR IS GOING ON IN SECTOR HILLSIDE 210. IT'S A REAL TRAGEDY. ACCORDING TO SOME EYE WITNESSES, A BERG COMMANDO, I REPEAT, A BERG COMMANDO, MADE...UH-OH, HERE'S A NEW DEVELOPMENT-- A COMBAT ROBOT HAS JUST APPEARED FROM OUT OF NOWHERE!

MEANWHILE...

GREAT! THE COAST'S CLEAR!

DON'T MOVE!

OH, NO!

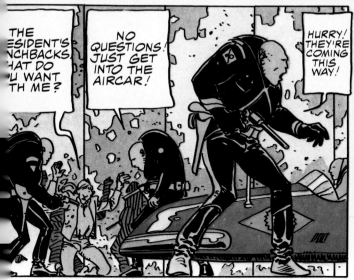

THE ESIDENT'S NCHBACKS, AT DO U WANT TH ME?

NO QUESTIONS! JUST GET INTO THE AIRCAR!

HURRY! THEY'RE COMING THIS WAY!

PFFF! IF THE PRESIDENT IS INVOLVED IN ALL THIS, I MIGHT AS WELL GIVE UP! IF HE WANTS THE INCAL, HE CAN HAVE IT!

19

CHAPTER THREE
HIS HIGH OPHIDITY

DEAR VIDFANS, WE'RE RIGHT INSIDE THE FLYING PALACE WHERE THE PRESIDENTIAL CLONING--THE 9TH AS YOU WELL KNOW--IS CURRENTLY UNDER WAY. THE INCOMING AND OUTGOING BODIES ARE IN PLACE SURROUNDED BY THE WONDERFUL TECHNO MACHINES.

THE NEW BODY IS MAGNIFICENT. OVER 7 FEET TALL...220 POUNDS OF PURE MUSCLE...IN TOP SHAPE!

...25...24... 23... 22...

IT'S SLOW!

...21...20...19...

YOUR HIGH OPHIDITY IS GOING TO HAVE TO WAIT ONLY A FEW MOR SECONDS.

HUNCHLEY, DO YOU HAVE ANY NEWS ABOUT THE INCAL AND THAT JOHN DIFOOL CHARACTER?

...18... 17... 16...

UP TO MY NECK IN IT... UP TO MY NECK...!

HE'S HERE, YOUR HIGH OPHIDITY, BUT HE DOESN'T SEEM TO HAVE THE INCAL ON HIM.

...15... 12... 1C

WHAT?!

SEARCH THE ENTIRE SECTOR. AND MAKE HIM TALK!

...9...8...

UNDERSTOOD. I SHALL PERSONALLY TAKE CARE OF THIS, YOUR HIGH OPHIDITY!

...7... 6... 5... 4...

IN THREE SECONDS...

IN THE CLONING CHAMBER, UNDER THE EYES OF THE TECHNO SCIENTISTS, THE ARISTO GUESTS, AND MILLIONS OF VIDFANS GLUED TO THEIR HOLO-TVS, THE MIRACLE OF THE TRANSFER TAKES PLACE...

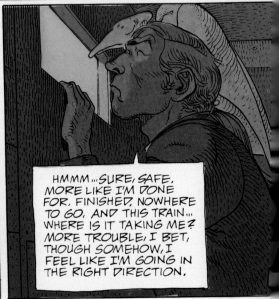

NOW, LET'S LOOK AT THIS LITTLE MARVEL. PFFT... AT LEAST, IT'S NOT BLINDING ME ANYMORE.

A SIMPLE CRYSTAL PYRA-MID... NOTHING SPECIAL ABOUT IT EXCEPT THAT GLOW... AND *YET*...

AND YET, SINCE IT WAS INSIDE ME, I'VE FELT LIKE...

I'M SURE THAT THE AN-SWER TO ALL MY QUESTIONS IS INSIDE THIS LITTLE PIECE OF GLASS!

INCAL... WHAT ARE YOU?

OOOH!

I AM THE INCAL!

YOU HAVE FINALLY DECIDED TO ASK A QUESTION!

?!!!

I HAVE BEEN MADE THUS... I NEVER SPEAK UNLESS CALLED UPON... YET OUR TIME IS LIMITED...

AND WE BOTH HAVE MUCH TO DO...

AMAZING! NOW, I GET IT! IT'S A MINATURIZED PHO-TONIC COMPUTER!

YOU ARE WRONG, JOHN DIFOOL! YOU HAVE NOT UNDERSTOOD ANYTHING! I AM NOT A COMPUTER. *I AM ALIVE*, JUST LIKE YOUR-SELF! AND THE POWERFUL WEBS OF FATE HAVE BROUGHT US TOGETHER SO THAT JUSTICE BE SERVED!

HEY! WAIT A MINUTE! I'M ONLY A CLASS-B INVESTIGATOR! I DON'T HAVE ANYTHING TO DO WITH JUSTICE!

BESIDES, I'VE GOT THE PRESIDENT'S HUNCHBACKS, THE ROBOCOPS AND THE MUTANTS FROM THE VENTILATION SHAFT ON MY TAIL!

I KNOW ALL THIS! THAT IS WHY I MUST TRANSFORM YOU!

AAAH! NO! I DON'T WANT TO BE TRANS-FORMED! I'M HAPPY THE WAY I AM, THANKS!

26

NONSENSE, YOU DO NOT KNOW WHO YOU ARE!

OKAY, SINCE YOU KNOW SO MUCH, TELL ME HOW TO ESCAPE FROM THE PRESIDENT AND ALL THE OTHERS. TELL ME WHERE YOU COME FROM, AND WHERE THIS TRAIN'S GOING ...TELL ME!

WE DO NOT HAVE THE TIME! ALL YOUR QUESTIONS WILL BE ANSWERED WHEN THE TIME COMES!

THE ONLY IMPORTANT QUESTION IS -- WHO, TRULY, IS JOHN DIFOOL? WHICH FORCES US TO CONSIDER- HOW MANY IS JOHN DIFOOL?

THAT'S THE DUMBEST QUESTION I'VE EVER HEARD!

WAIT UNTIL YOU KNOW THE ANSWER BEFORE PASSING JUDGEMENT I WILL...

HEEYY...

...SHOW YOU!

ERKK!

MY GOD!

HERE IS A PART OF THE ANSWER.

YOU T... THAT QUES... WA... NOT... DU... AF... A... N... YOU ... TW...

AND NOW YOU ARE THREE.

AND THE LEGS MAKE FOUR!

ONLY NOW CAN YOU ASK THE QUESTION...

WHO IS JOHN DIFOOL?

IT'S ME!

IT'S ME!

IT'S ME!

IT'S ME!

TIME PASSES... SLOWLY, JOHN DIFOOL REGAINS CONSCIOUSNESS.

HMMMM... HOW LONG WAS I OUT?

WAS IT A DREAM? I... NO! MY HEAD... THE INCAL!

MY HEAD! MY LEGS! I'M BACK IN ONE PIECE!

CROOT

DEEPO! YOU LOOK TERRIFIED! DON'T BE AFRAID! IT'S ME, JOHN DIFOOL!

CROOT ROOOTK...

MY GOD, I FEEL STRANGE! THERE'S A FEELING INSIDE... AS IF MY HEART WAS SHINING... GLOWING...

CROOT! IT'S THE INCAL!

I KNOW WHAT YOU MEAN! REMEMBER, IT WAS IN MY STOMACH NOT TOO LONG AGO!

BUT, DEEPO... YOU TALK!

ME, TALK? YEAH, I GUESS I DO... IT JUST KIND OF CAME TO ME. BY THE WAY, WHERE ARE WE GOING?

ER... I DON'T... NO, SUD-DENLY I KNOW.

WE'RE INSIDE A FUNERAL TRAIN HEADED FOR TECHNO CITY! HEY! EVEN THE PRESIDENT CAN'T GET INSIDE TECHNO CITY!

SOUNDS LIKE FUN TO ME.

SO, WHAT ARE WE GOING TO DO IN THAT DREARY HOLE?

I DON'T KNOW YET, DEEPO. BUT I HAVE THE FEELING WE'RE NOT GOING TO LIKE IT... ONE WORD KEEPS POPPING INTO MY MIND... THE INCAL... THE DARK INCAL!

CHAPTER FOUR
TECHNO TECHNIQUE

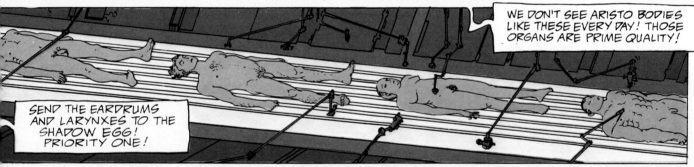

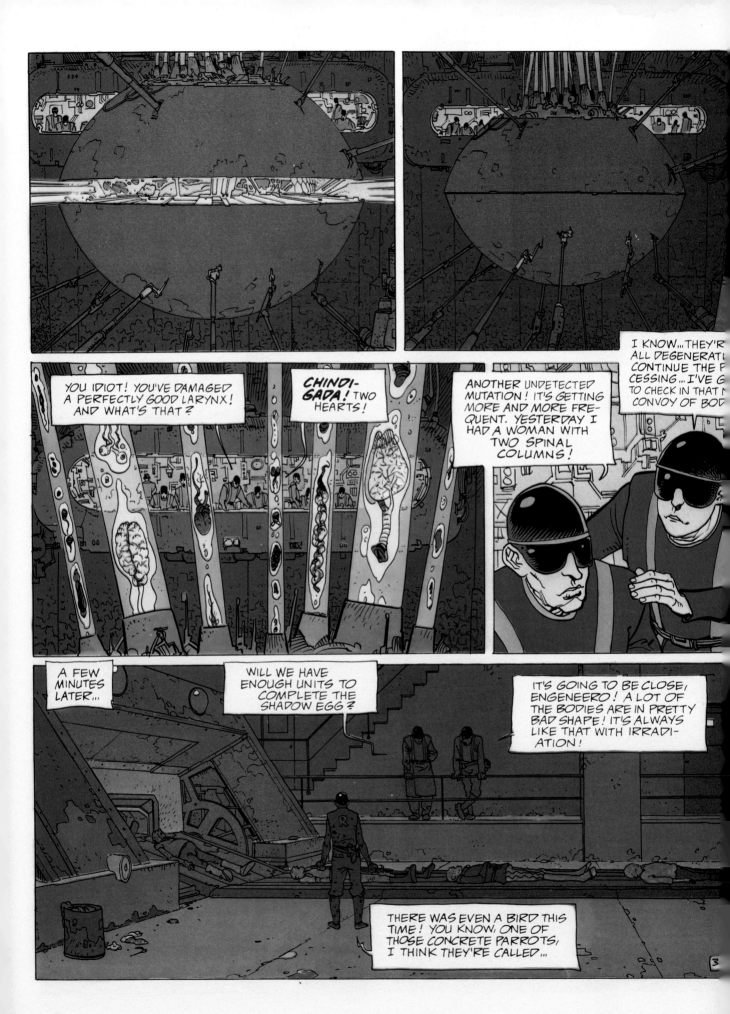

CHAPTER FIVE
THE META-BARON

FINALLY, YOUR STER RAT HOLE!

WELCOME TO AMOK H.Q.1 *META-BARON!*

? 'THE...THE META-BARON?!

SO YOU'RE AMOK'S QUEEN? HERE ARE MANY DARK AND STRANGE TALES ABOUT YOU UP THERE!

THERE ARE MANY TALES ABOUT YOU DOWN HERE. BUT WHO CARES? THEY'LL SOON HAVE REASON ENOUGH TO FEAR ME.

COME CLOSER AND LET US TALK. YOU RETIRED TEN YEARS AGO. I WENT TO A GREAT DEAL OF TROUBLE TO GET YOU TO COME OUT OF YOUR LAIR. I'M SORRY.

GODMOTHER... GODMOTHER... CAN HE BRING *HIM* BACK ALIVE? FOR ME.

STOP SHOUTING IN MY EAR, WOLFHEAD! SIT!

WOLFHEAD WANTS REVENGE!

YOU CLAIM TO HOLD MY SON PRISONER? WHERE IS HE? IS HE STILL...

...ALIVE? OF COURSE, MY DEAR META-BARON, OTHERWISE, WHAT BARGAINING POWER WOULD I HAVE?

PULL BACK THE CURTAIN! HE MUST SEE!

38

UNLESS...

HERE'S THE FILE ON JOHN DIFOOL.

I WANT THIS MAN BROUGHT TO ME IN 24 HOURS. DEAD OR ALIVE!

WOLF-HEAD--

--GIVE THE FILE TO THE META-BARON!

OF COURSE! IT'S THAT PETTY PRIVATE EYE WANTED BY ALL THE ROBOCOPS IN TOWN. IT WON'T BE EASY, ESPECIALLY WITH THE STATE OF EMERGENCY. AND ALL THE RIOTS...

JOHN DIFOOL. HMM... IS FACE LOOKS FAMILIAR.

THAT IS NOT A PROBLEM! HE'S NO LONGER IN THE CITY.

HE'S GONE NORTH... TO TECHNO CITY!

BRING HIM BACK ALIVE! I'VE GOT A SCORE TO SETTLE WITH HIM!

SHUT UP, WOLF-HEAD!

TECHNO CITY? THAT WON'T BE EASY EITHER.

THAT VERMIN'S NEST... NOW, I UNDER-STAND THE REASON FOR YOUR BLACKMAIL.

NO FEE WOULD HAVE BEEN HIGH ENOUGH TO MAKE ME TAKE THIS JOB. NOW, I HAVE NO CHOICE... I'LL DO IT! BUT BE WARNED, IF SOMETHING HAPPENS TO MY SON, I'LL KILL YOU! ALL OF YOU! ALL!

END OF
BOOK ONE

 discovered French comics through Moebius' western series, **Blueberry**. I had never heard of him before, but I was immediately seduced by his cinematographic style. After having seen his work, I felt I had just met a friend. So when I began working on the **Dune** project, I asked him to come and work with me.

We worked eight hours a day on that film, for months and months. It was a wonderful time, during which we formed a solid friendship. We were both in total resonance with each other. Moebius drew so fast that it was just incredible. To work with him was better than working with the most sophisticated cameras. His pen almost miraculously created all the travelings, the panning shots, the zooms I wanted. It gave me a full register of all the emotions I wanted to see on the faces of my actors. Through the three thousand

plus drawings he did for **Dune,** I could feel just as if I had actually shot the picture. Anyone looking at his work would feel that they had experienced the film as fully as if they had seen it on a screen in a theater.

Then, when the project fell apart, we naturally felt frustrated, incomplete. So, as soon as I hit upon the idea of **The Incal,** I knew that only Moebius could draw it. **The Incal** could be what **Dune** never was. In a way, you could say that we reinvested in **The Incal** the frustration we felt at not being able to make **Dune.**

The Incal began as a dream, one where I was aware that I was indeed dreaming. In that dream, I was sitting in some nebulous space, when

I asked to see a vision of my innermost being. Two imbricated pyramids appeared. Then, I said to myself, it is good to see what my innermost being looks like, but it is not yet enough. I must now become one with that pyramid. But when I tried to achieve this, I felt as if my brain was exploding with light, and then I woke up.

So the Incal first appeared to me in a dream. Then, I began writing a story in which I wanted to tell how someone became the Incal. To write that story, I tried to ignore my powers of logic and reasoning, and instead place myself in a position of receiving the story directly from my subconscious. I have always felt that true, magical art is something that you receive, that is being given to you.

Before I began writing **The Incal,** I reread most of Mickey Spillane's books, because I wanted to have his sense of pacing. **Kiss Me Deadly,** the Aldrich film adapted from a Spillane novel, was a definite influence on me. Like **The Incal**, it begins with a small discovery, and ends in an apocalyptic fashion, except of course that my apocalyptic ending is a positive one. Moebius is the one who made me slow down, arguing sometimes that we should give some breathing space to the readers.

Although it took Moebius and me almost ten years to complete **The Incal,** I don't think that that time had any real impact on the story. I knew its general direction from the start, with all its essential details. Other things, that were still hidden in my subconscious, surfaced as we went. I think that any solid work requires patience anyway. When you truly love something, time doesn't matter. I believe there is a deeper meaning to things that is not affected by the passing of time. For a human being, it is that part of himself that he carries within him from cradle to grave. The same is true of stories like **The Incal,** for which years are like minutes.

My method of collaboration with Moebius is rather unique. I search for the story almost as if I was in a trance. I think of myself as if I were knocking on the gates of heaven, which open, and then someone gives me the story, which I humbly accept. Afterwards, I don't write it. I tell it to Moebius, and while I tell him, I act it out, I mime it. I come up with the names of the characters and the places, which come out of the same creative trance, and he takes notes and asks me questions. With his superhuman rapidity, he sketches the story as I go along, and I can see the pages appear almost simultaneously. Because he is so fast, and I am naturally inventive, it only takes us four days to do an entire book.

Afterwards, we talk about the dialogue. In my opinion, the writer should never impose his views of the dialogue on the artist, because sometimes a drawing will be enough to convey what you want to say, and you don't need words. The writer should never obstruct the artist's work, or hamper his imagination. Because of this unique form of collaboration, when Moebius draws **The Incal,** he can do a page a day, almost directly in ink, like some Japanese artists.

BOOK TWO THE BRIGHT INCAL
CHAPTER ONE OVE TENEBRAE

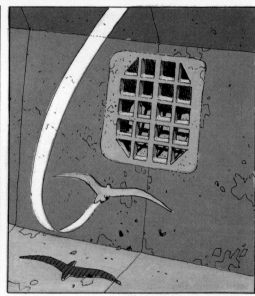

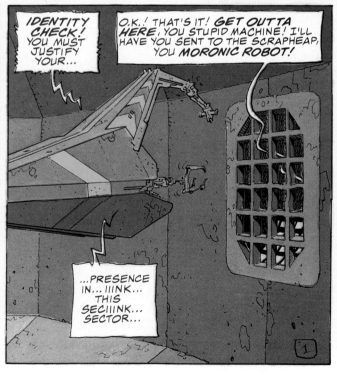

KRASK

CROOOTK!?

IIINK... PRESENCE IN THIS SECTOR...

SUDDENLY, A VIOLENT GUST OF AIR CATCHES THE UNFORTUNATE DEEPO.

!?

A VENTILAT... OH, MY GO... I'VE HAD... NOW!

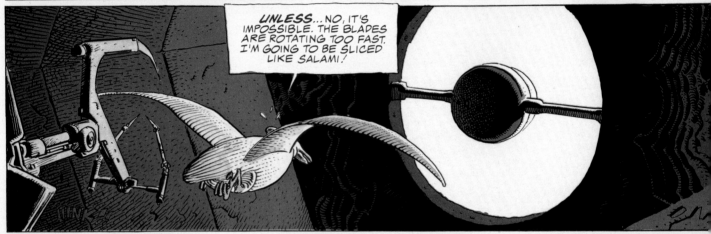

UNLESS... NO, IT'S IMPOSSIBLE. THE BLADES ARE ROTATING TOO FAST. I'M GOING TO BE SLICED LIKE SALAMI!

IDENTIT...INNNK!

I'VE GOT TO MAKE IT! I USED TO BE GOOD AT THIS IN THE OLD DAYS, WHEN I WAS WITH THAT GANG OF FLEDGLINGS AT THE HELIPORT. GOING THROUGH A SET OF ROTATING BLADES.

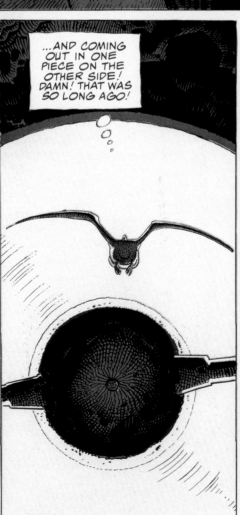

...AND COMING OUT IN ONE PIECE ON THE OTHER SIDE! DAMN! THAT WAS SO LONG AGO!

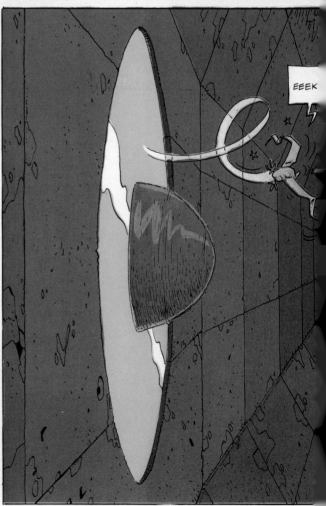

EEEK

HURRAY! I GOT DINGED UP A BIT, BUT I MADE IT!

JUST LIKE THE GOOD OL' DAYS!

ANYWAY, THAT JUNKPILE DIDN'T FOLLOW. LOOKS LIKE I'M FINALLY OUT OF TROUBLE!

OKAY, NOW TO GET MY BEARINGS, EVALUATE THE SITUATION, AND TRY TO FIND JOHN DIFOOL!

MAYBE I...ARGH! THAT'S...HORRIBLE!

THERE! JOHN DIFOOL! THAT LUNATIC, THE TECHNO-POPE, GOT HIS HANDS ON HIM!

NO-BROTHERS, GRAND MOMENT FINALLY ARRIVED!

O, INCAL, DON'T LET ME DOWN NOW!

OUR UNION WITH THE GREAT DARKNESS WILL BEAR ITS DARK FRUIT TONIGHT!

FISTS RAISED! RESOUNDING CHORUS! TECHNO MADNESS!

THIS IS OUR DAY OF VICTORY AND GRATIFICATION! OUR ENEMY, THE *BRIGHT INCAL*, WHO PRETENDED TO ILLUMINATE US, BUT IN FACT WAS ONLY *BLINDING US...*

HOLY CONCRETE! THE TECHNO-POPE AND ALL THE TECHNOS HAVE GONE CRAZY!

...WITH HIS ACCURSED LIGHT. THAT ENEMY IS NOW HERE. **POWERLESS!**

PRISON INSIDE T STUPID A STUBBO BIO-UNI

WE SENT A COMBAT ROBOT TO THE VERY CENTER OF THE CITY TO SEIZE HIM, BUT INSTEAD, THIS FOOL CHOSE TO THROW HIMSELF INTO THE LION'S DEN!

INCAL, SINCE YOU'RE SO CLEVER, SEND ME BACK TO MY GOOD OL' CONAPT WITH A GOOD OLD BOTTLE OF OUISKY AND MY FAITHFUL BOX OF SPV. PLEASE, INCAL!

BUT BEFORE WE BEGIN THE TECHNO DISMEMBERMENT, WE ARE GOING TO UNLEASH THE FIRST *SHADOW EGG*, WHOSE FATHER IS THE *DARK INCAL* AND WHOSE MOTHER, THE *GREAT DARKNESS*. A PRELUDE TO A MILLION OTHERS, TO BE SENT THROUGHOUT THE UNIVERSE.

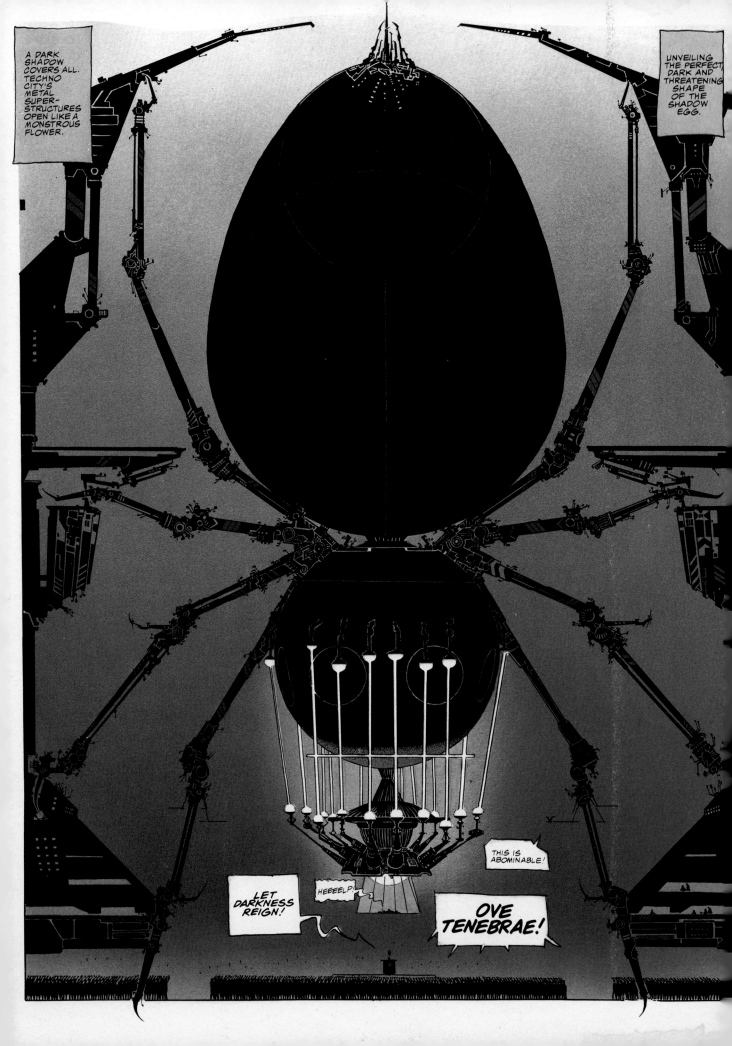

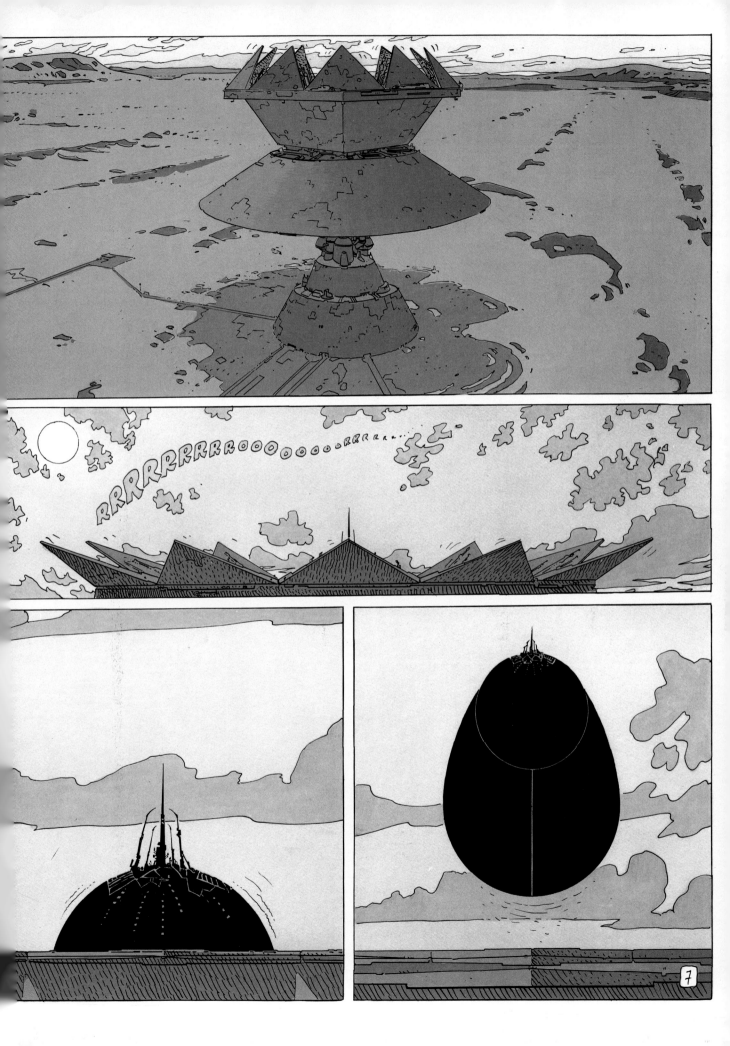

RRRRRRRRRROOOOOOOORRRRr....

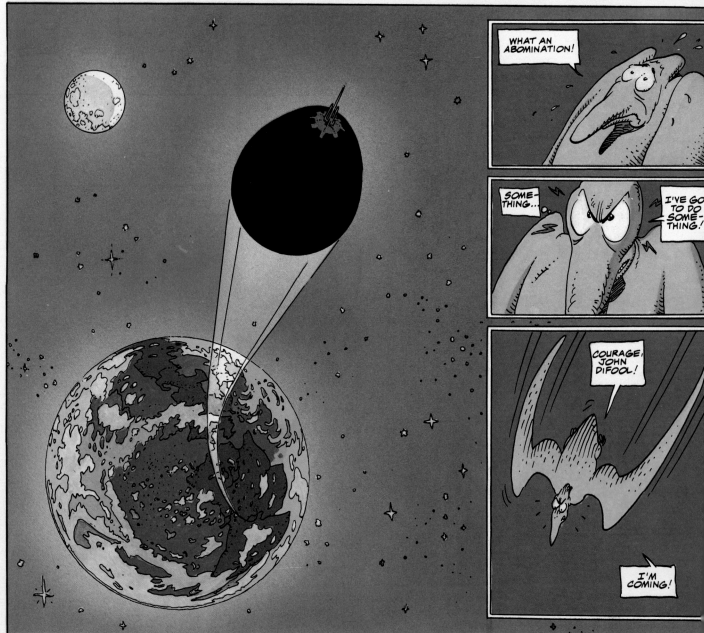

CHAPTER TWO
PANIC IN THE INTERNAL EXTERIOR

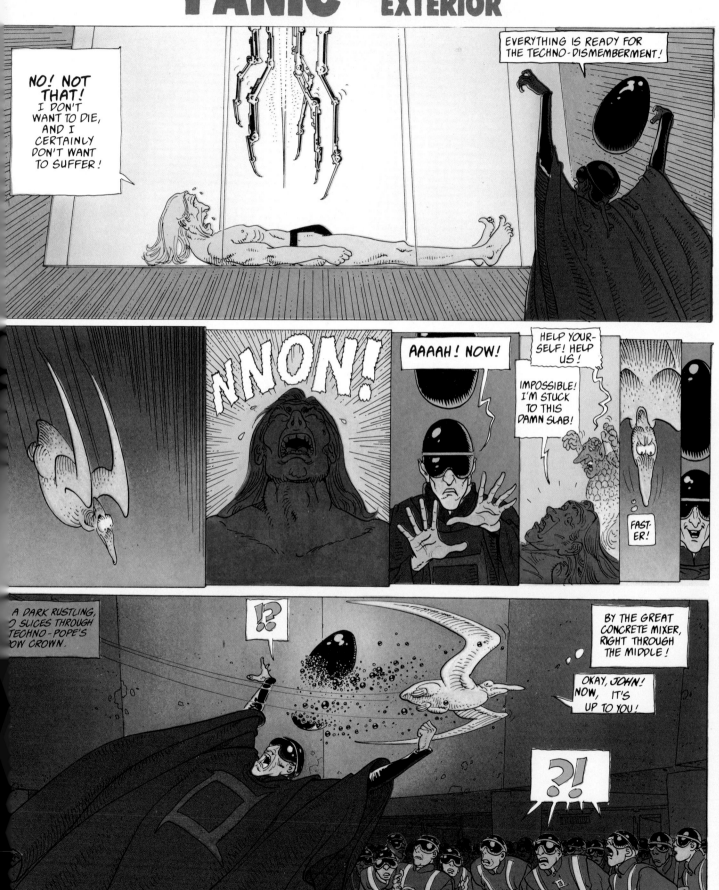

UNLEASH
YOUR
TECHNO
POWERS !

UP THERE! ON TOP OF THIS SPHERE! THERE'S A TRAPDOOR!

GREAT! THE KEY WORD HERE IS "TRAP," I SUPPOSE?

THEY'RE ESCAPING!

THE PEGAZ! RELEASE THE PEGAZ!

HUR

LOOKS LIKE A NEW HELL DOWN THERE!

IF YOU DON'T SHUT THIS DOOR FAST, IT'LL BE A LOT WORSE UP HERE!

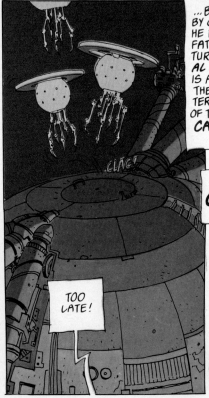

CLAC!

TOO LATE!

...BUT NO MATTER... BY CLOSING THAT DOOR, HE HAS SEALED HIS FATE! THERE IS NO RETURN FROM THE INTERNAL EXTERIOR! AND HE IS AWAITED THERE BY THE SACRED AND TERRIBLE GUARDIAN OF THE DARK INCAL--THE CARDIOCLAW!

THE CARDIOCLAW!

THE...TH CARDIO CLAW

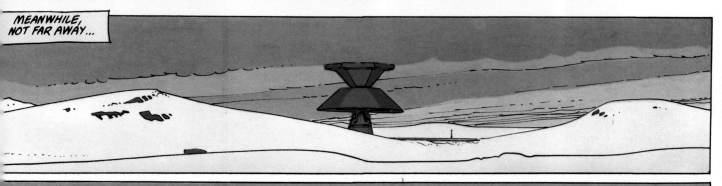

THE DETECTION MONITOR IS CERTAIN! WHAT WE'RE LOOKING FOR IS INSIDE THAT BUILDING OVER THERE!

HAVEN'T WE HAD ENOUGH LOSSES, ALREADY, CHIEF?

IT LOOKS LIKE A REAL FORTRESS, CHIEF!

YOU'RE NOTHING BUT A BUNCH OF MURGS! REMEMBER THAT THE PROTOQUEEN HERSELF IS SUPERVISING THIS COMMANDO ON COSMOVIDEO. THIS WILL MAKE AN EXCELLENT OBSERVATION POST.

AND TRY TO BEHAVE LIKE REAL BERG HEROES, FOR GOD'S SAKE!

NO NEED TO SWEAR, CHIEF!

STOP! SILENCE! TOTAL IMMOBILITY!

WHAT'S GOING ON, CHIEF?

IT'S AN INDIGENOUS HUMAN!

ALONE?

WHAT SHOULD WE DO?

HE'S GOING TO ALERT THE OTHERS!

LET'S ELIMINATE HIM! AT MY COMMAND, SHOOT HIM DOWN! READY. AIM.

CHAPTER THREE
ANIMAH !

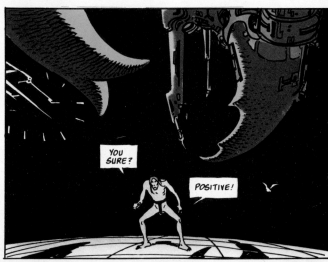

17

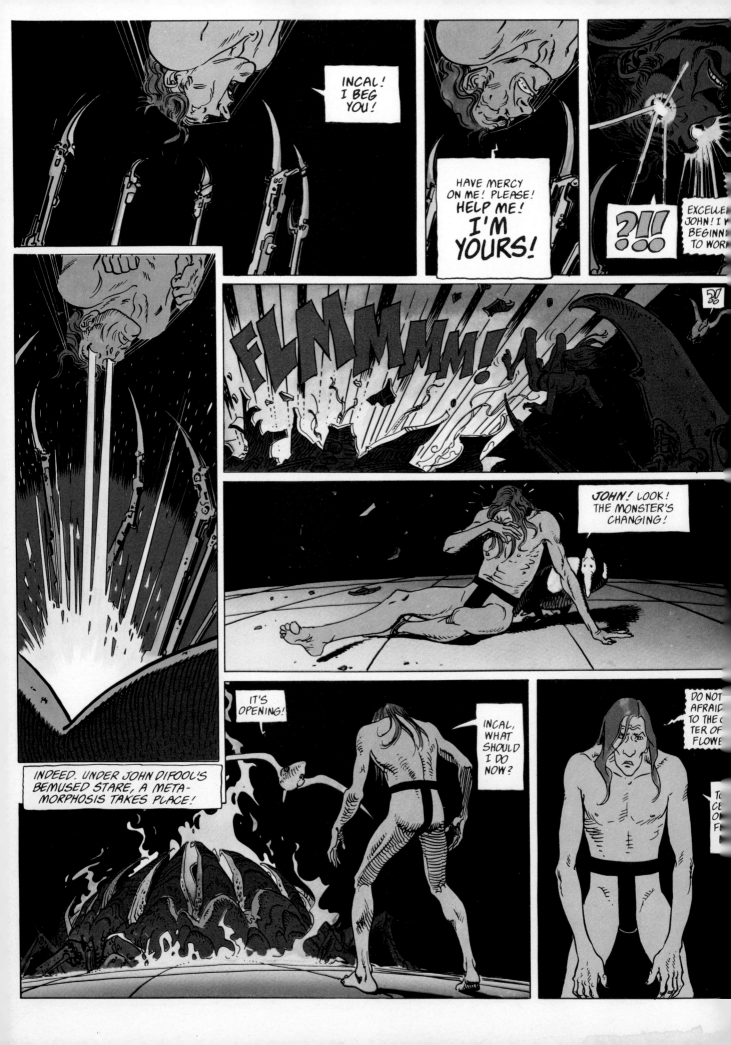

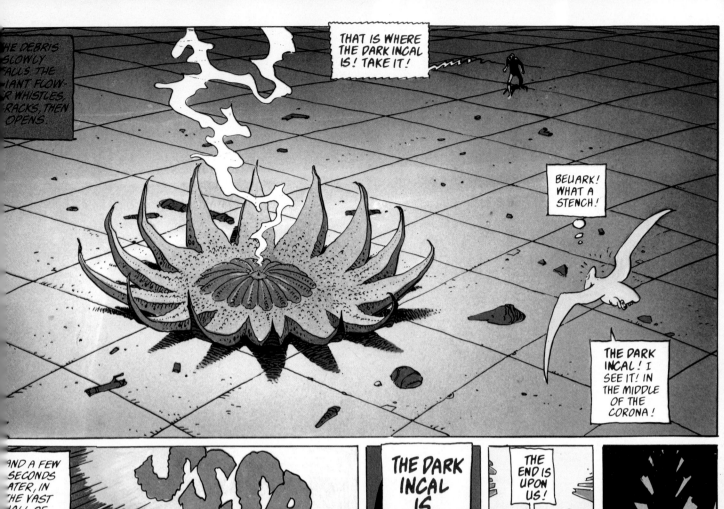

THE DEBRIS SLOWLY FALLS THE GIANT FLOWER WHISTLES, CRACKS, THEN OPENS.

THAT IS WHERE THE DARK INCAL IS! TAKE IT!

BEUARK! WHAT A STENCH!

THE DARK INCAL! I SEE IT! IN THE MIDDLE OF THE CORONA!

AND A FEW SECONDS LATER, IN THE VAST HALL OF THE TECHNO TEMPLE...

MOTHER DARKNESS! IT'S IMPOSSIBLE! THE CARDIOCLAW HAS BEEN DEFEATED!

THE DARK INCAL IS LOST!

THE END IS UPON US!

13

LET ME THROUGH!

YOUR HIGH OPHIDITY! THERE'S BEEN A DISASTER! TECHNO CITY HAS JUST BEEN DESTROYED!

WHAT'S THE MATTER, MY GOOD HUNCHLEY?

CURSES! HOW AM I SUPPOSED TO ENJOY MYSELF IN THE MIDST OF THIS VERITABLE AVALANCHE OF MIS-HAPS? DARN!

RIOTS! PLOTS! BERG COMMANDOS! TREACHERY! AND NOW TECHNO CITY GOES BOOM!

AND THAT *JOHN DIFOOL* IS STILL ON THE LOOSE! I MUST DO SOME-THING, LEST I LOSE MY GORGEOUS LOOKS! YES, DO SOMETHING, BUT WHAT? *WHAT?*

YOUR HIGH OPHIDITY, I...

BROOOMMMMM

CALL THE *EMPERORATRIX*, YOUR HIGH OPHIDITY! THE TOTALLY FULFILLED PERFE BEING, MASTER-MISTRESS OF THE HUMAN EMPIR

CALL... THAT?

MEANWHILE, FAR AWAY, IN THE FROZEN, SNOWSWEPT WILDER-NESS...

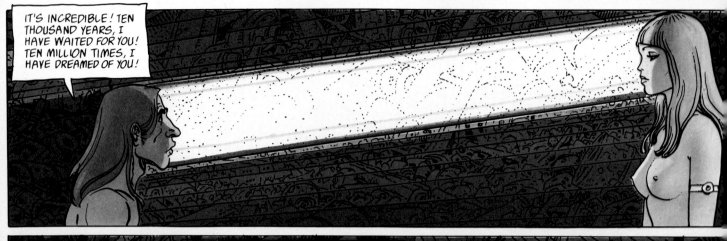

IT'S INCREDIBLE! TEN THOUSAND YEARS, I HAVE WAITED FOR YOU! TEN MILLION TIMES, I HAVE DREAMED OF YOU!

WHAT'S YOUR NAME?

ANIMAH!

WHEN WILL I SEE YOU AGAIN?

IDIOT! NEVER! ASSHOLE! [YOU] GAVE HER THE [INC]K INCAL! JUST [LIK]E THAT! A [PRECI]OUS TREASURE [THAT] NEARLY COST [Y]OUR LIFE!

YOU HEARTLESS MONSTER! YOU'RE LETTING HER GO! WELL, THEN, THERE'S NOTHING LEFT FOR US BUT TO DIE OF SORROW, BROKEN-HEARTED.

BITCH! GIVE ME BACK MY INCAL!

BELOVED! COME BACK! DON'T LEAVE ME LOST OUT HERE!

COME BACK!

WHOOPS!

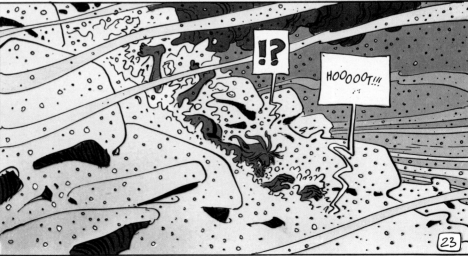

!?

HOOOOOT!!!

23

NO! POOR OLD DEEPO!

SO THAT'S WHERE YOU WERE?

CROOOT...

YUP. THAT'S WHERE I WAS!

JOHN DIFOOL! HOLY CONCRETE! I DO BELIEVE WE'VE MANAGED TO SURVIVE ONE MORE TIME!

I'M GOING TO TAKE YOU BACK INSIDE, WH THERE'S SHELTER... YOU'RE NOT HURT? NOTHING BROKEN

I'M O.K., I'M O.K. I JUST NEED TO G THIS DAMNED BLA GOOK OFF ME, THAT'S ALL!

WE WERE SAVED BY... BY HER, THE ONE...

JOHN!

BEHIND YOU!

?!

WHAT THE HELL IS IT THIS TIME?

I AM THE META-BARON AND I HAVE BEEN SENT TO THIS PLACE TO KILL JOHN DIFOOL!

CHAPTER FOUR
NEURAZTENIK CLASS STRUGGLE

DEAR HOLO VIDFANS, WE'RE PRIVILEGED TODAY TO WITNESS THE MOST SPECTACULAR CARNAGE. OVER A MILLION RIOTERS RUSH TOWARDS THE GAPING HOLE OPENED BY THE NUCLEO-EXPLOSION IN THE FLANK OF THE FLYING PALACE.

WHY NOT TAKE COVER BY TAKING THE PALACE UP AGAIN?

IMPOSSIBLE! SEVERAL STABILIZING UNITS WERE DAMAGED BY THAT DAMNED NUCLEO!

IN THE NAME OF THE BLUE SEDENTARISTS, **ONWARD!**

IONIST PHALANXES WITH ME!!

GODMOTHE... EVERYTHING GOING WEL...

GOOD! DO... THEM BR... SPACE...

GIMME A TIGHTER SHOT ON THE BOMBING!

ADD A FEW TEARS...

DON'T FORGET THE FAKE BURNS!

DEAR VIDFANS! YOU'RE ONE LUCKY GROUP, SNUGLY LOCKED INSIDE YOUR CONAPTS, WATCHING THIS EXCEPTIONALLY HUGE CITY RIOT ON YOUR HOLOVIDS.

BUT HERE, MEN ARE FIGHTING. FOR THEIR FREEDOM, THEIR RIGHT TO MOVE CLOSER TO THE SURFACE. THEIR RIGHT TO FREE SPV. AND SIMPLY, THEIR RIGHT TO RIOT!

NOW, LET'S GO TO A DIRECT FEED OF THE RIOTERS' ATTEMPT TO INVADE THE PRESIDENTIAL PALACE. BUT FIRST, THESE COMMERCIAL MESSAGES!!!

DAMN! THEY'RE USING TECHNO EQUIPMENT! WE'VE BEEN BETRAYED!

ALERT HIS HIGH OPHIDITY! THE SITUATION IS BECOMING INCREASINGLY CRITICAL!

THE ONLY THING LEFT IS TO LAUNCH THE HYPER-HALO!

BUT... THAT WOULD BE HORRIBLE!

LOOK! UP THERE! WHAT'S THAT GLOWING SPIRAL PATTERN THAT JUST APPEARED?

SHIT! IT'S THE HYPER-HALO! WE'RE DOOMED!

ZLGBZZZGB

GET BACK!

RUN!

NO! KEEP CLIMBING! AMOK HAS A PLAN!

AMOK SOLDIERS, PREPARE FOR ACTION! INDIVIDUAL INVERSORS AT THE READY!

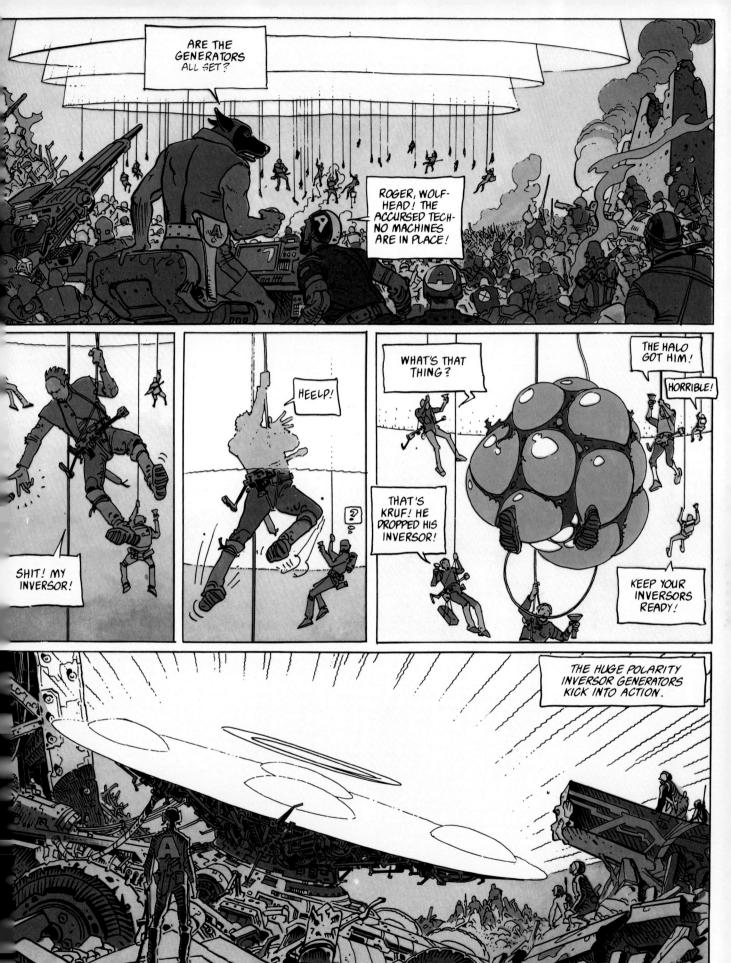

MEANWHILE, NEAR THE FLYING PALACE'S SUMMIT...

AHAHAH!...

TEE HEE HEE! YOU'RE TICKLING ME!

MORE DRINKS! MORE DRINKS!

LET'S SMOKE SOME GRASS!

LET'S SNIFF SOME POWDER!

MMM...THIS DRAGONFLY SOUFFLE IS SUPURB!

SUPREME!

WOW! THERE ARE SOME ABSOLUTELY DIVINE KILLINGS ON THE HOLO!

IF CITY RIOTS DIDN'T EXIST, SOMEBODY WOULD HAVE TO INVENT THEM!

YOUR...YOUR HIGH...

?

YOUR HIGH OPHIDITY!

THE...THE REBELS HAVE SUCCEEDED IN DEFLECTING THE HA...HALO!

WHO SAID YOU COULD DISTURB MY TEA PARTY DOG!

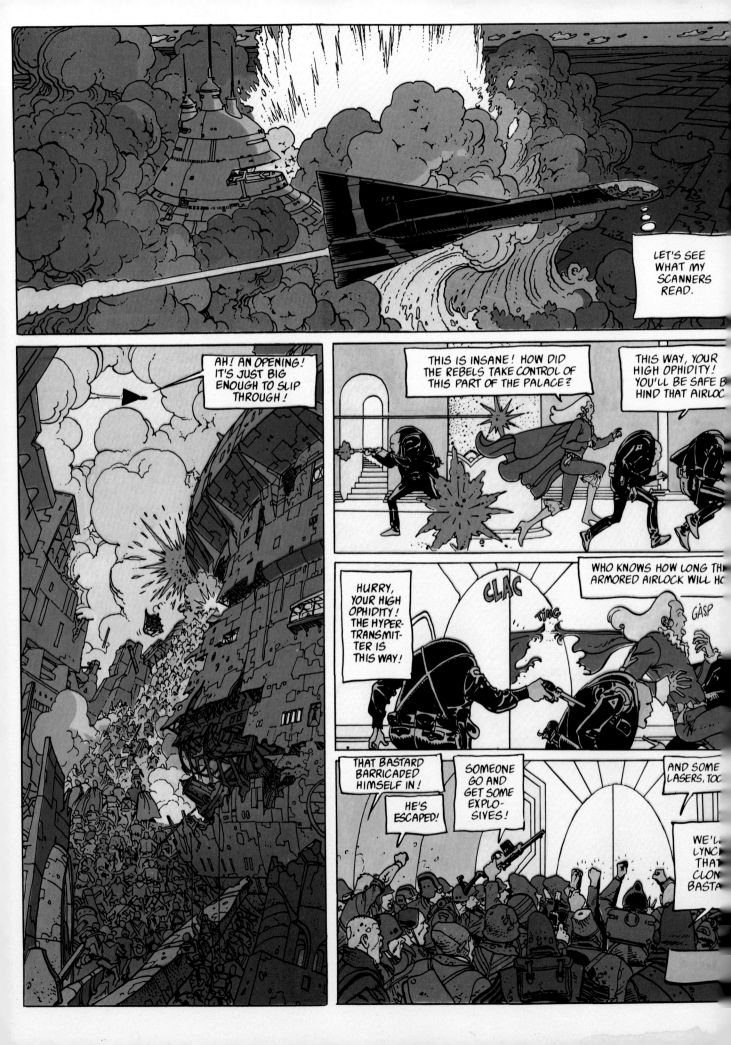

CHAPTER FIVE
THE EMPERORATRIX

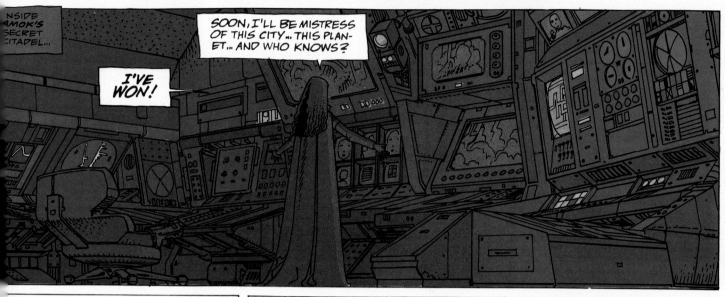

INSIDE AMOK'S SECRET CITADEL...

SOON, I'LL BE MISTRESS OF THIS CITY... THIS PLANET... AND WHO KNOWS?

I'VE WON!

...AT PUPPET PRESIDENT IS NOW POWERLESS THERE IN HIS FLYING PALACE, AND SOON MY ...EL PAWNS WILL BE GROVELING AT MY FEET.

WITH THE BRIGHT INCAL IN MY POWER, I'LL NEED ONLY TO UNITE IT WITH THE DARK INCAL THAT FOOLISH TECHNO-POPE BELIEVES HE HOLDS...

AND MY POWER WILL VIRTUALLY BE LIMITLESS!

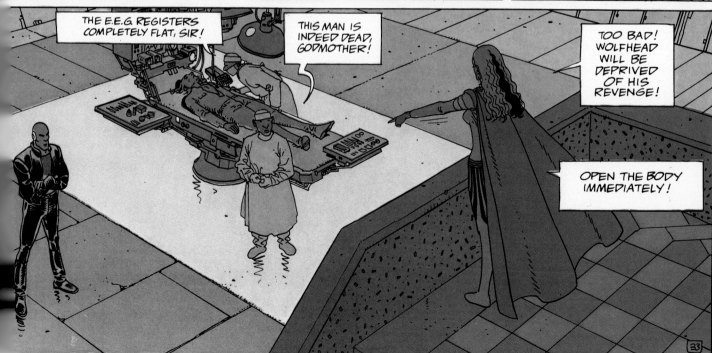

THE E.E.G REGISTERS COMPLETELY FLAT, SIR!

THIS MAN IS INDEED DEAD, GODMOTHER!

TOO BAD! WOLFHEAD WILL BE DEPRIVED OF HIS REVENGE!

OPEN THE BODY IMMEDIATELY!

23

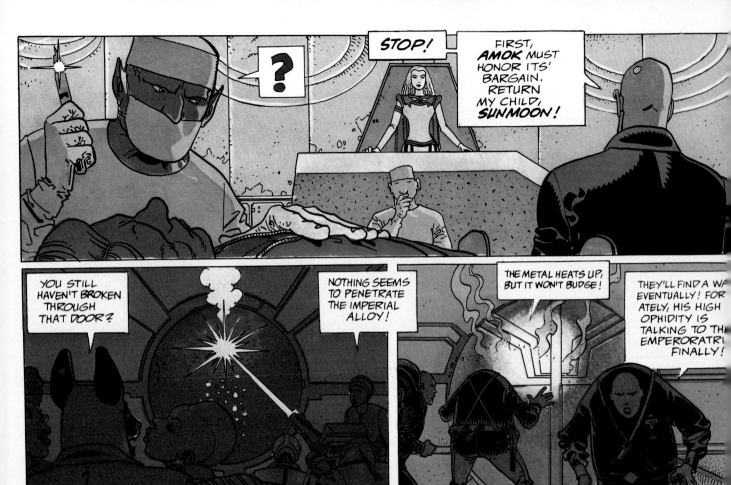

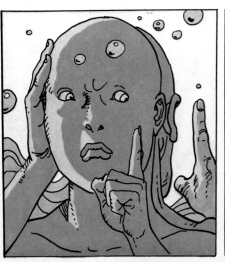

WAIT! SOMETHING THAT I DON'T UNDERSTAND IS HAPPENING. I FEEL AN UNKNOWN ENERGY IN YOUR SECTOR. A GROWING CONSCIOUSNESS SUPERIOR TO OURS.

HE...HE MUST HAVE FELT THE INCAL!

ANOTHER RIOT PROGRAM! THIS IS GETTING BORING!

THE BAZOOKA'S NOT GOOD ENOUGH! BRING SOME ANTI-MATTER MINES!

MEANWHILE, IN THE CONAPTS...

BOY, THAT WOLF-HEAD'S A SCREAM!

ON THE CONTRARY, NED! I FIND IT SUPER-INTERESTING! THEY'RE TRYING TO LYNCH THE PRESIDENT!

RETURN HIM? NEVER! FIRST, HE'S NOT YOUR CHILD, AND YOU KNOW IT! BESIDES HE'S A MONSTER

SUN-MOON!

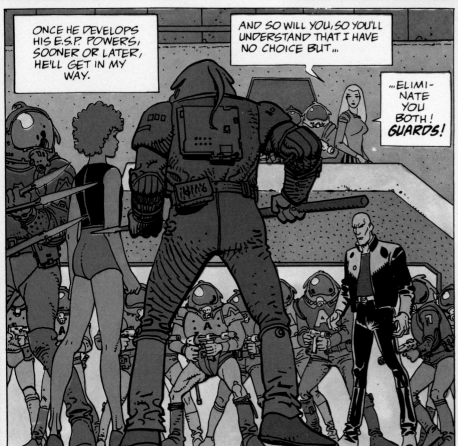

ONCE HE DEVELOPS HIS E.S.P. POWERS, SOONER OR LATER, HE'LL GET IN MY WAY.

AND SO WILL YOU, SO YOU'LL UNDERSTAND THAT I HAVE NO CHOICE BUT...

...ELIMI-NATE YOU BOTH! GUARDS!

KILL THE META-BARON! KILL SUNMOON! OPEN UP THAT BODY!

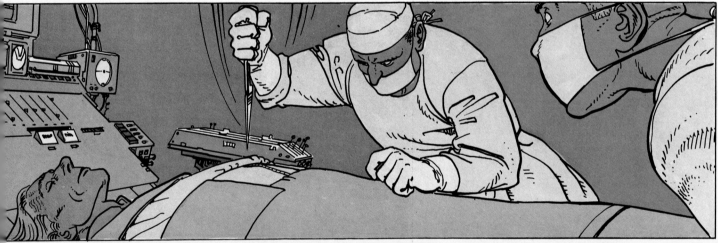

THE IMPERIAL FLEET HAS SET OUT TO DESTROY THE BERGS AND THAT MYSTERIOUS BLACK EGG. IT'S THE END OF A LONG, UNIVERSAL PEACE. WE'RE NOW ENTERING OUR FIRST GREAT INTERGALACTIC WAR.

LISTEN! NOW HERE IS WHAT YOU ARE GOING TO DO...

37

SOON AFTER...

BMM

ATTACK!

WATCH OUT FOR THE HUNCHBACKS!

DIE!!

AAARGH!

THIS WAY!

THIS IS THE ONLY PLACE HE COULD BE HIDING!

THE PRESIDENT!

THE BASTARD! HE KILLED HIMSELF BEFORE WE COULD GET HIM!

DEAD!

LET'S RIP APART HIS CARCASS!

SHUT UP! ALL OF YOU! THERE'S SOMETHING HERE I DON'T LIKE...

DEAR VIDFANS! YOU MAY ALL BE IN YOUR CONAPTS SNUG AS A BUG IN A RUG, BUT HERE, IT'S A SUSPENSEFUL MOMENT! WOLFHEAD'S NOSE IS POINTING IN ALL DIRECTIONS! HE SMELLS A TRAP!

CHAPTER SIX THE ACID LAKE

GODMOTHER! ALL IS LOST! THEY'VE LAUNCHED THE NECROPROBE!

THE NECRO-PROBE!

!!?

THE NECROPROBE! SO THEY DARED UNLEASH THAT ABOMINATION, CREATING A NEW REIGN OF TERROR UPON THIS WORLD! AS FOR ME ... I MUST ACCEPT MY FAILURE!

WHAT HAPPENED TO THE GUARDS?

THEY MET WITH THREE WARRIORS!

BUT WE STILL HAVE ONE TRUMP CARD LEFT--YOU, JOHN DIFOOL! IN THEORY, YOU HAVE THE TWO IN-CALS IN YOUR POSSESSION, HERE'S WHAT WE'RE GOING TO DO!

SORRY. I NO LONGER HAVE THE DARK INCAL!

WHAT? WHERE IS IT?

GAVE IT TO WOMAN!

GAVE IT TO A WOMAN?

?

?

?

?

HER NAME IS ANIMAH!

HER! I SUSPECTED AS MUCH! NICE MOVE! I NO LONGER HAVE ANY CHOICE FOR MY NEXT STEP.

ANIMAH! MY MOTHER... FINALLY!

ANIMAH! THE QUEEN OF THE RATS!

SO!

WITHOUT THE DARK INCAL, THE BRIGHT INCAL IS POWERLESS AGAINST THE NECROPROBE, IF YOU ALL WANT TO LIVE, WE MUST STAY TOGETHER AND UNITE OUR FORCES!

FOLLOW ME!!

41

BUT WE'RE GETTING FURTHER FROM THE SURFACE!

OUR SALVATION LIES BELOW!

HEY! THE EARTH'S SHAKING!

BUT THERE'S NOTHING BELOW, EXCEPT FOR THE GREAT ACID LAKE!

THAT'S WHAT EVERYONE BELIEVES!

WA
OF
FA
IN
RO

IN FACT, THE LAKE IS THE HIDDEN DOORWAY TO A VAST WORLD AT THE CENTER OF THIS PLANET. THE GREAT CRYSTAL CAVES, PYRAMID ISLAND. IT'S FROM THIS SECRET WORLD THAT ANIMAH AND I COME!

ARE YOU SISTERS?

VERY PERCEPTIVE! YES, WE ARE! WE WERE THE GUARDIANS OF THE TWO INCALS. BUT THE GREAT DARKNESS CAME AND LURED ME TO ITS SIDE. I THEN STOLE THE DARK INCAL AND CAME TO THE SURFACE WORLD TO GAIN POWER!

I TRADED IT TO THE TECHNOS FO THEIR MACHINES! THEN, I TRIE TO STEAL THE BRIGHT INCAL, B JOHN DIFOOL INTERVENED, A CREATED THE FATAL INTERFER THAT LAUNCHED THE WHOLE CRIS

AMOK'S SECRET BUNKER!

I ALMOST THOUGHT I WOULD SUCCEED, BUT IN THE END, I FAILED! NOW, I MUST RETURN BELOW, WHATEVER THE PRICE ...

...THE TWO INCALS MUST BE REUNITED!

LOOK THE NECRO PROBE SINGLE HANDE DESTR ING OUR ARMY

ARE YOU THERE, MY FAITHFUL SERVANTS?

CRRRK

WHO GOES THERE?

IT IS I,... TANATAH!

CAREFUL, GODMOTHER

SCCROOMM!

?

THE,... THE TUNNEL IS COLLAPSING!

THE COLLAPSE HAS OPENED A HOLE IN THE WALL!

oOOK!,,

THERE! THE ACID LAKE!

MY POOR SERVANTS!

AND THE META-SKIFF!

ALL IS NOT LOST YET! THERE'S ANOTHER ENTRANCE TO THE WORLD BELOW ON THE OTHER SIDE OF THE LAKE!

JOHN DIFOOL! I WAS STARTING TO GET WORRIED!

LOOK! IT'S DEEPO!

A BUNCH OF ROCKS FELL ON THE SKIFF! THAT REALLY SHOOK ME UP!

DAMN! THE ENGINE'S RUINED!

43.

HELP ME PUSH!

NO ENGINE?

WE'LL SHOOT SOME MAGNA-LINES ONTO THE SUPERSTRUCTURE, THEN WE'LL PULL OURSELVES ACROSS!

SOON AFTER...

IT'S WORKING! WE SHOULD BE ON THE OTHER SIDE IN LESS THAN TEN MINUTES!

IT'LL BE CLOSE! THE NECRO-PROBE MIGHT CATCH UP WITH US ANY SECOND!

FASTER!

DAMN! THE ACID IS EATING AWAY AT THE META-SKIFF'S HULL!

AND THAT'S NOT ALL! I FEEL A CURRENT CARRYING US AWAY!

IMPOSSIBLE! THE ACID LAKE DOESN'T HAVE...

OVER THERE LOOK!

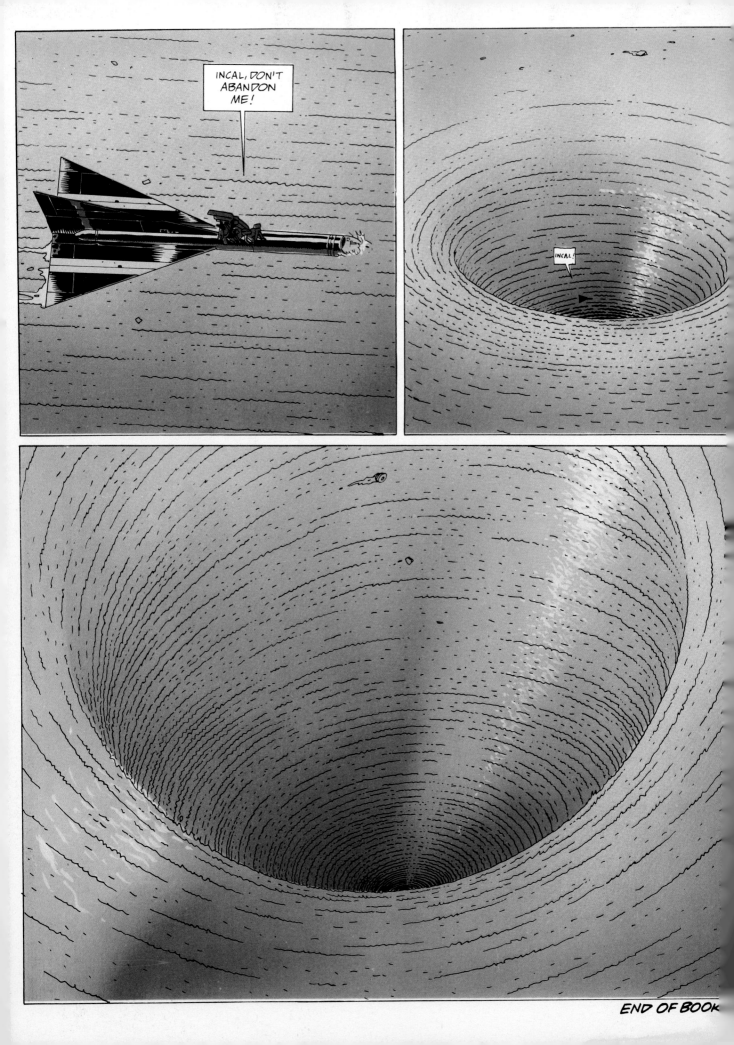

END OF BOOK